MY CLARA

A Fairy Tale Written by

Rachel Wilson

Illustrated by

Rebecca Evans

ISBN# 1-930710-32-1
Copyright ©2000 Veritas Press

Veritas Press
1250 Belle Meade Drive
Lancaster, PA 17601

First edition

MY CLARA

A Fairy Tale Written by
Rachel Wilson

Illustrated by
Rebecca Evans

Veritas Press

The spring sun was a bit hot in the snapdragon patch. Clara was to scrub the steps spit spot, wash the linens and hang them in the sun, and then drill her spelling.

Yet Clara was in
the snapdragon
patch. She did
love the smell of
the snapdragons
and to nap on the
splendid grass.

She did love the song of the thrush. Yet as Clara was skipping in the patch, the thrush was not singing. She had to stop and be still. The thrush was missing. She was still for a long spell, but there was no song in the shrub.

Clara did miss the song of the thrush. Then there was a sad shrill from the shrubs. Clara ran to the bush and there sat the thrush on a twig. The thrush was not singing for she had a ring stuck on her bill. Clara did stretch to snatch the ring from the thrush.

The thrush did not twitch for she did watch Clara napping in the snapdragon patch as the thrush was singing. Clara did strip the ring off her bill, and the thrush sprang off the bushes onto the grass. Clara was checking the status of the ring that she did snag. The ring struck her eye with its flash.

"My Clara,
My Clara,"
sang the thrush.
"What!?"
said Clara.
"My Clara, My
Clara," sang the
thrush and did flit
along the path.
Clara stuck the
ring in the pocket
of her smock and
ran to the thrush.

The thrush
was hopping
up the path.
"My Clara,
My Clara,"
sang the thrush,
and did skip into
the bushes.
Clara sped along
with the thrush as
she was hopping
up the path,
across the
snapdragon patch
wall, and into the
thicket. Clara had
been in the
thicket, but not
on this path.

The thrush still was hopping on and on and Clara with her. As they trod across the wet moss into the black walnut thicket, Clara did thrust off her snug clogs.

Then Clara did spot a big black walnut fed by a spring. It was the biggest black walnut. It was to this that the thrush led her. The thrush was hopping onto the bottom twig of the walnut and sang, "My Clara, My Clara."

With a swish the
thrush did step
into a crack at the
back of the black
walnut. Clara did
skip to the walnut
and did step into
the crack as well.
She had to squish
to fit. There were
small steps which
led her up within
the big black
walnut.

The steps did stop at the walnut's attic. The sun fell from the cracks in the big black walnut and did splash upon a box of swell dresses and a chest of rings and things. "My Clara, My Clara" sang the thrush. Clara did spin to hush the thrush, but with a rush the thrush did switch into a lass! She was a nix in a splendid dress.

She had a gloss like the rings in the chest; and the nix did dwell in the attic of the spring-fed big black walnut. Clara was glad the lass had led her to the attic of the big black walnut, but she had to rush back to her snapdragon patch. She had steps to scrub, linens to wash, and spelling to drill.

The nix sang a lot as a thrush in the snapdragon patch when Clara was to scrub the steps, wash the linens, and drill her spelling. Then Clara did visit the nix's attic. Clara did love to put on the nix's splendid dresses and rings, and sing with the skillful nix lass in the attic of the spring-fed big black walnut.